Weather Fun

with

MOTHER GOOSE

Compiled by Stephanie Hedlund
Illustrated by Jeremy Tugeau

visit us at www.abdopublishing.com

Looking Glass Library™ is a trademark and logo of Magic Wagon.

Printed in the United States of America, North Mankato, Minnesota.
102010
012011
 This book contains at least 10% recycled materials.

Compiled by Stephanie Hedlund
Illustrations by Jeremy Tugeau
Edited by Rochelle Baltzer
Cover and interior layout and design by Abbey Fitzgerald

Library of Congress Cataloging-in-Publication Data

Weather fun with Mother Goose / compiled by Stephanie Hedlund ; illustrated by Jeremy Tugeau.
    v. cm. -- (Mother Goose nursery rhymes)
  Contents: Nursery rhymes about weather -- When clouds appear -- If chickens roll -- Rain before seven -- Rain, rain, go away -- As the days grow longer -- Winter's thunder -- The north wind doth blow -- Fair today, rain tomorrow -- Here we go round the mulberry bush -- A sunshiny shower -- Blow, wind, blow! -- It's raining, it's raining -- The winds they did blow.
  ISBN 978-1-61641-147-3
 1. Nursery rhymes. 2. Weather--Juvenile poetry. 3. Children's poetry. [1. Nursery rhymes. 2. Weather--Poetry.] I. Hedlund, Stephanie F., 1977- II. Tugeau, Jeremy, ill. III. Mother Goose.
  PZ8.3.W3739 2011
  398.8 [E]--dc22
                    2010024699

Contents

Nursery Rhymes
About Weather

Since early days, people have created rhymes to teach and entertain children. Since they were often said in a nursery, they became known as nursery rhymes. In the 1700s, these nursery rhymes were collected and published to share with parents and other adults.

Some of these collections were named after Mother Goose. Mother Goose didn't actually exist, but there are many stories about who she could be. Her rhymes were so popular, people began using Mother Goose rhymes to refer to most nursery rhymes.

Since the 1600s, nursery rhymes have come from many sources. The meanings of the rhymes have been lost, but they are an important form of folk language. Nursery rhymes for weather are stormy, sunny, and funny.

When Clouds Appear

When clouds appear like rocks and towers,
The earth's refreshed by frequent showers.

If Chickens Roll

If chickens roll in the sand,
Rain is sure to be at hand.

Rain Before Seven

Rain before seven,

Fine before eleven.

Rain, Rain, Go Away

Rain, rain, go away,
Come again another day.

13

As the Days Grow Longer

As the days grow longer
The storms grow stronger.

Winter's Thunder

Winter's thunder
Is the world's wonder.

The North Wind Doth Blow

The north wind doth blow,

And we shall have snow,

And what will poor robin do then?

Poor thing!

He'll sit in a barn

And keep himself warm

And hide his head under his wing.

Poor thing!

Fair Today, Rain Tomorrow

This little man lived all alone,

And he was a man of sorrow;

For, if the weather was fair today,

He was sure it would rain tomorrow.

Here We Go Round the Mulberry Bush

Here we go round the mulberry bush,
The mulberry bush, the mulberry bush,
Here we go round the mulberry bush,
On a cold and frosty morning.

This is the way we wash our hands,
Wash our hands, wash our hands,
This is the way we wash our hands,
On a cold and frosty morning.

This is the way we wash our clothes,
Wash our clothes, wash our clothes,
This is the way we wash our clothes,
On a cold and frosty morning.

This is the way we go to school,
Go to school, go to school,
This is the way we go to school,
On a cold and frosty morning.

This is the way we come out of school,
Come out of school, come out of school,
This is the way we come out of school,
On a cold and frosty morning.

A Sunshiny Shower

A sunshiny shower

Won't last half an hour.

Blow, Wind, Blow!

Blow, wind, blow! And go, mill, go!

That the miller may grind his corn;

That the baker may take it,

And into bread make it,

And send us some hot in the morn.

It's Raining, It's Raining

28

It's raining, it's raining,
There's pepper in the box,
And all the little ladies
Are holding up their frocks.

29

The Winds They Did Blow

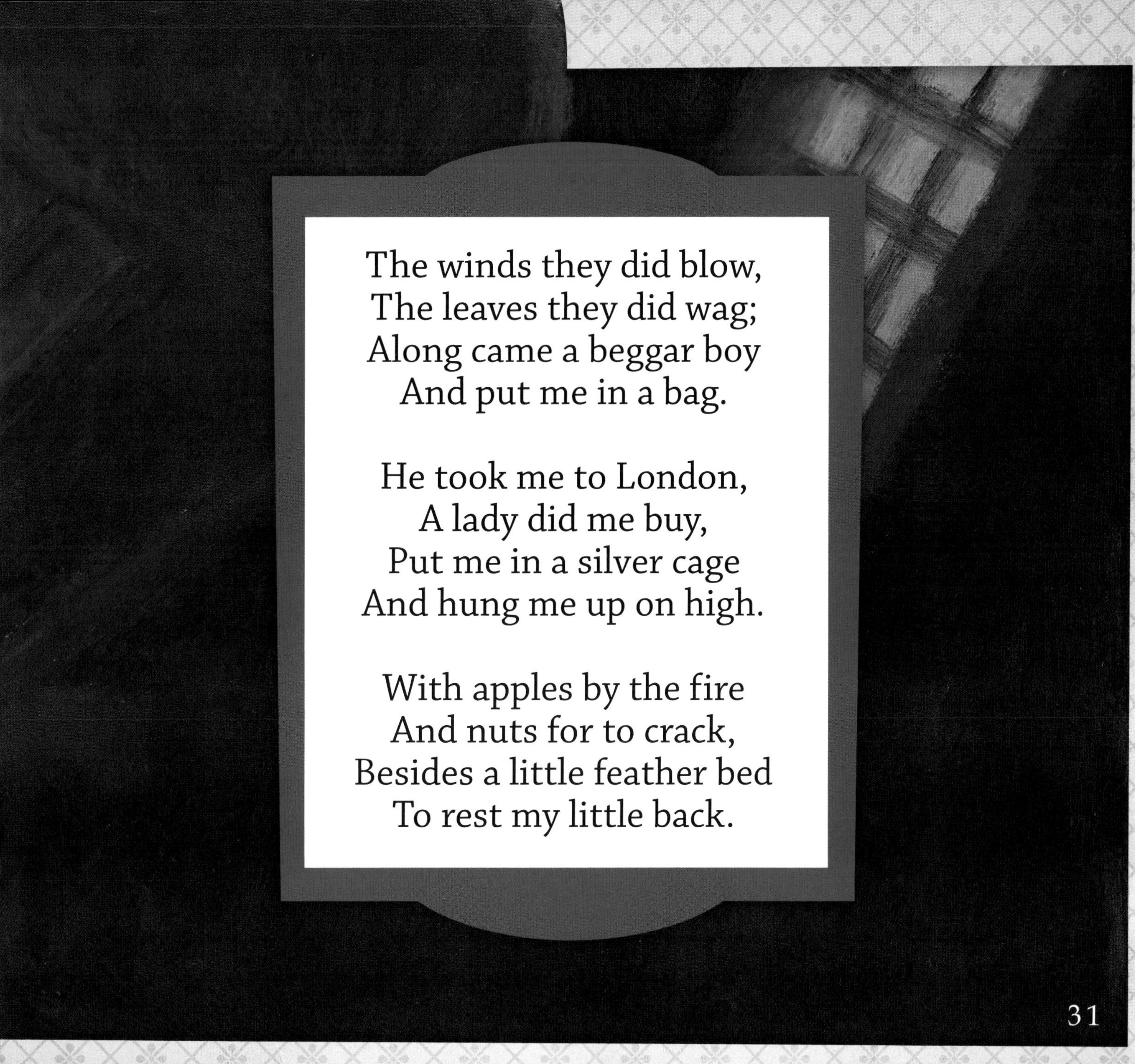

The winds they did blow,
The leaves they did wag;
Along came a beggar boy
And put me in a bag.

He took me to London,
A lady did me buy,
Put me in a silver cage
And hung me up on high.

With apples by the fire
And nuts for to crack,
Besides a little feather bed
To rest my little back.

Glossary

doth – an old way of saying do.

frequent – something that happens often.

frock – a woman's dress.

miller – a person who grinds grain into flour.

sorrow – a deep sadness or regret.

Web Sites

To learn more about nursery rhymes, visit ABDO Group online at **www.abdopublishing.com**. Web sites about nursery rhymes are featured on our Book Links page. These links are routinely monitored and updated to provide the most current information available.